Mine

by M.G. Higgins

ISBN-13: 978-1-62250-820-4
ISBN-10: 1-62250-820-3

Printed in Guangzhou, China
NOR/0716/CA21601271

20 19 18 17 16   3 4 5 6 7

I love Emma.

She is pretty. She is smart.

Emma is all I want.

She is all I need.

3

I drive Emma to the mall where she works.
I wrap my arm around her.
I like her close.

She takes a deep breath.
"Tyler," she says. "I want to hang with Lana tonight."

"Why?" I ask.

"Lana has problems," Emma says. "She wants to talk."

"But this is Saturday," I say. "Can it wait?"

"I never see Lana anymore. She is my best friend." We stop in front of the shoe store.

"I thought I was your
best friend," I say.
"And we have plans for tonight."

She moves out from
under my arm.
She heads to the store.

"Hey, wait," I say.
I hate when she turns her
back on me. I grab her hand.

"Let go," she says.
"I have to get to work."

My face heats up.
But I let her go.
"Fine. Whatever."

She looks sad and hurt.
I step up close and kiss her.
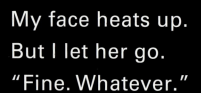
"Sorry. I love you."

She does not say it back.
My heart pounds.
"Do you love me?" I ask.
She barely nods.

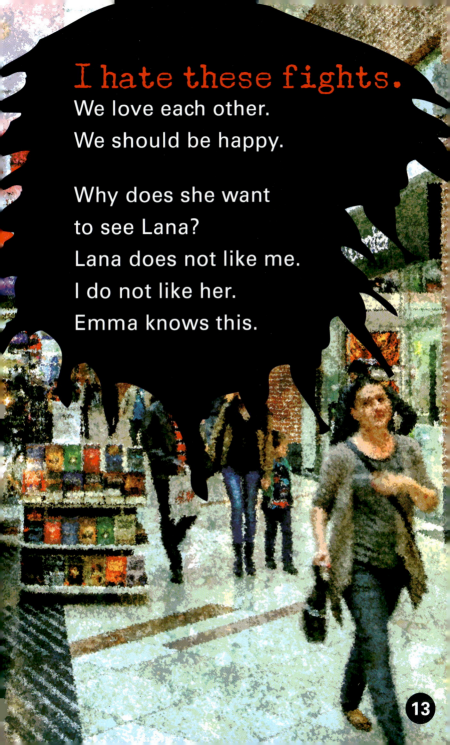

I hate these fights.

We love each other.
We should be happy.

Why does she want
to see Lana?
Lana does not like me.
I do not like her.
Emma knows this.

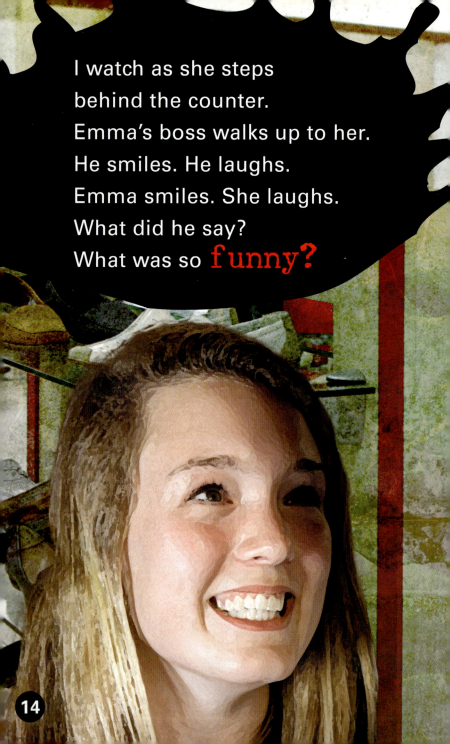

I watch as she steps
behind the counter.
Emma's boss walks up to her.
He smiles. He laughs.
Emma smiles. She laughs.
What did he say?
What was so funny?

Is he hitting on her?
Is she letting him?
I feel hot again.
I should go. I don't want trouble.
But my mind shuts off.
All I see is red.

I step into the store.
"Can I help you?" her boss says.
He is big and tall.
He crosses his arms.

I want to yell at him.
I want to punch him.
But I say, "No."

I glare at him and then at Emma.
I storm away.

Jealousy rages through me.
I do not know what to do.

I walk through the mall.
Finally, I pull out my phone
and text Emma.

Messages   Emma   Contact

He wants you.
I can tell.

She texts back.

He does not. He has a wife and kids.

Stay away from him.

How can I stay away from him? He is my boss.

You know how. Just do it. Do not be a b____.

I wait for her to text back.
She does not.

My hands shake. I am so **mad.**
I should drive home.
There are things to do.

But I text her again.
I text her over and over.
She does not text back, not once.
What is going on?

I think about Emma with her boss.
I think about Emma with other
guys. I even think about Emma
with Lana.
I hate what I see in my mind.

How can she do this?
She should stay away from them.
I am all she needs.

25

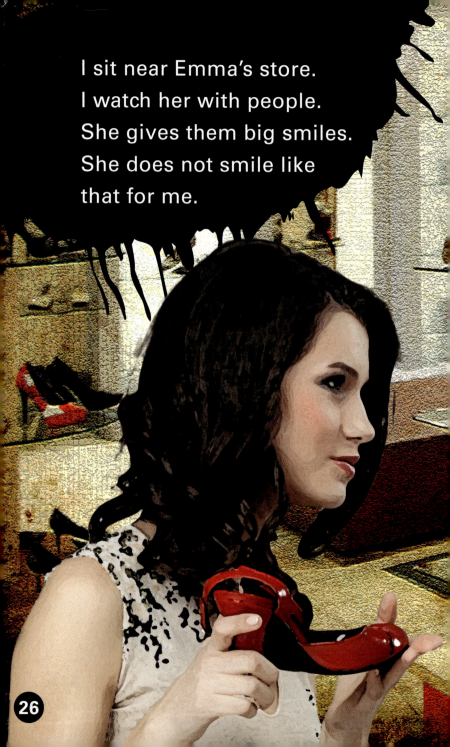

I sit near Emma's store.
I watch her with people.
She gives them big smiles.
She does not smile like
that for me.

I know I should trust her.
But how can I?
She is too pretty.
I fear I will **lose her.**

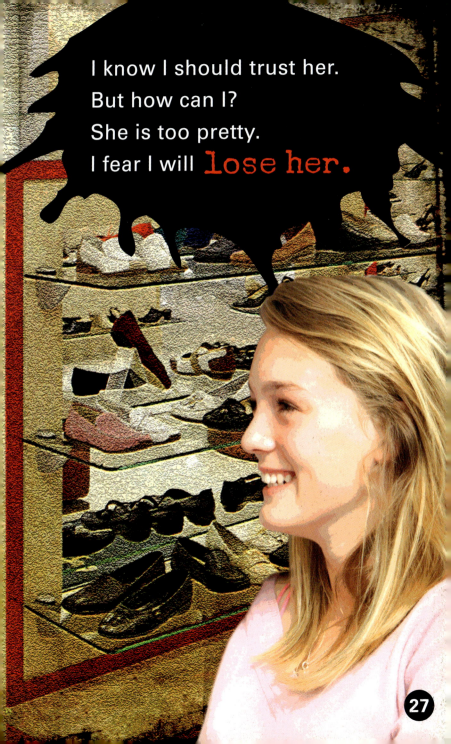

It is Emma's lunch break.
I follow her to the food court.
She eats by herself.
Good. I feel a little better.

I text her.
Hi. I love you.

She looks at her phone.
She does not text back.
Why not? What is going on now?

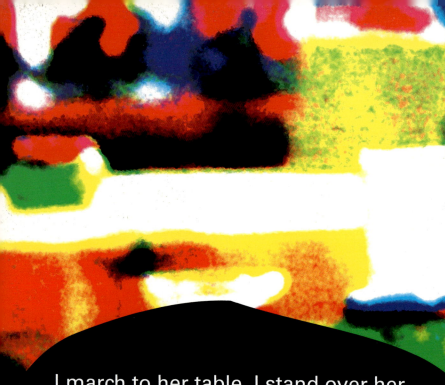

I march to her table. I stand over her.
She looks up. Her jaw drops.
"Tyler. What are you doing here?"

"We need to talk," I say.

"You sent me over 100 texts this
morning!" she says.

"And you did not text back,"
I say. "Why?"

She bites her lip.
"Let it go. Give me some space."
She looks away.

"Hey! Look at me!"
I grab her chin and twist it around.
"Why did you not text me?"

She jumps up from the table.
"Leave me alone."

She knows better than
to walk away.
I hold her by her arm.

"Stop it!" she yells.
She bats at my hand.

"Emma," I say.
I want to cry. I want to scream.
"Do not break up with me!
If you do I will kill myself."

She slips from my grasp.

She runs.

"Emma!"

I start to go after her.

But a mall cop sees me.

He walks toward me.

I leave the mall.

I drive home.

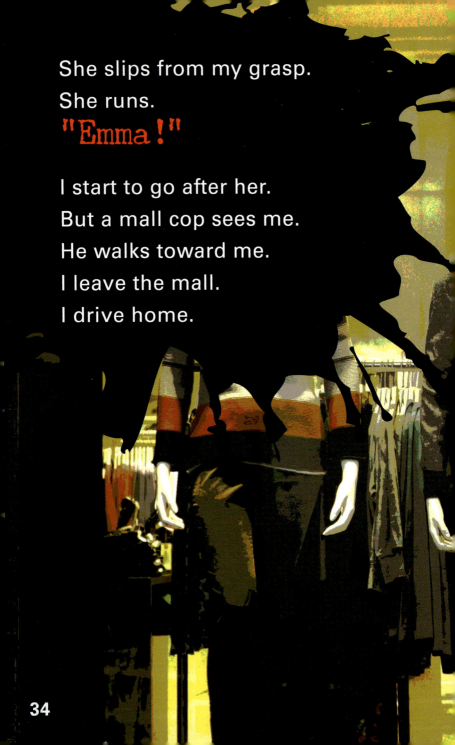

It is a bad night.
It is a bad weekend.

I call Emma again and again.
I text her over and over.
I do not hear a thing.

I go to her house.
I pound on her door.
"Emma!"
No one comes.

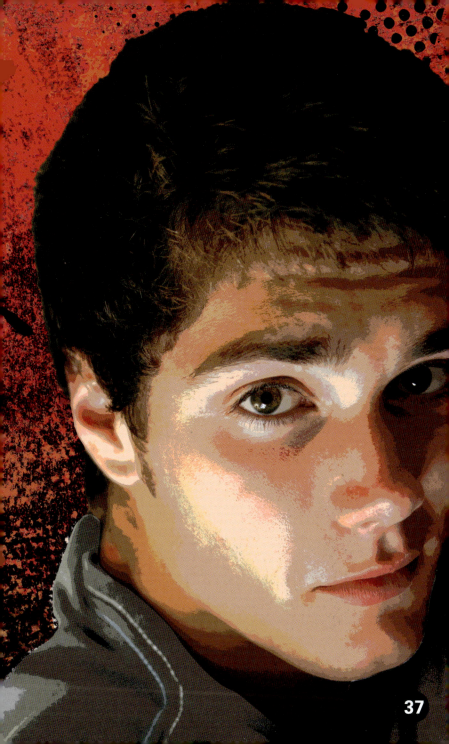

Sunday there is a knock at
my front door.
I run to answer it.
But it is not Emma. It is a cop.

"Are you Tyler Hash?" he says.

"Yeah," I say.

"You are under arrest," he says.

I stare at him.
"Why? What did I do?"

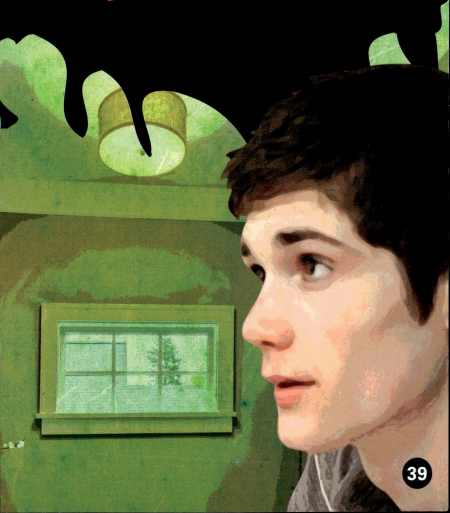

"Stalking. Verbal abuse.
Physical abuse. Threats."

He gets out his **handcuffs.**
"Turn around."

I do what he says. But crap.
This has something to do
with Emma.
But I don't know what.

"Emma is my girlfriend," I say.
He pulls the cuffs tight.
They hurt.
"We love each other."

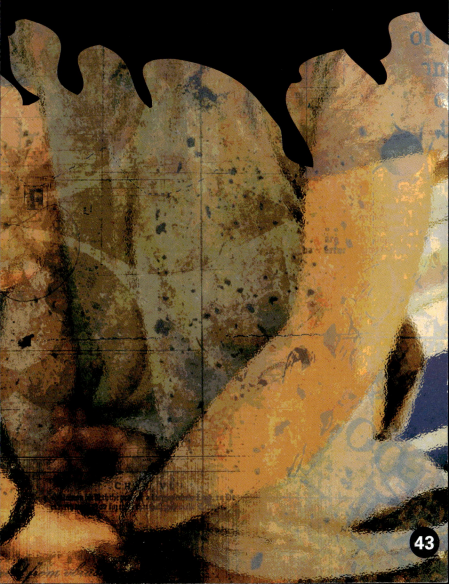

"**Harassment** is against the law," he says.
He shoves me into his car.

Harassment?

I think about it as he drives.

Did I stalk her?
Abuse her?
Threaten her?
I pound my head against
the window.

I love Emma.
She is all I want.
She is all I need.
What have I done?

46